Stewie BOOM!
and
Princess Penelope

Handprints, Snowflakes
and
Play-dates

Written by
Christine Bronstein

Illustrated by
Karen L. Young

To: Everyone who has ever felt different.

Published in 2018 by Nothing But The Truth, LLC
NothingButtheTruth.com

Stewie BOOM! and Princess Penelope: Handprints, Snowflakes and Play-dates and Nothing But The Truth name and logo are trademarks of Nothing But The Truth Publishing, LLC.

Also available in ebook.

Library of Congress Control Number: 2017905394

Stewie BOOM! and Princess Penelope: Handprints, Snowflakes and Play-dates
By Christine Bronstein
Illustration by Karen L. Young
Edited by Summer Laurie
ISBN 9780997296273 (paperback)
ISBN 9780997296280 (hardcover)
ISBN 9780997296297 (ebook)

Printed in the United States of America
2018
First Edition

Understanding Autism Spectrum Disorder

Every second, our brains work to understand the things we see, smell, hear, taste, touch and experience. But when someone's brain interprets these things differently, it can make it harder for them to communicate and know what others are trying to say to them. It can also make everyday sights and sounds very intense. But, just like everyone else, people with autism spectrum disorder (ASD) come in all shapes, sizes and colors. Some have incredible strengths and some have difficulty with everyday tasks.

My name is Princess Penelope and I like stuffies,
playing make believe with my friends and baking.
My brothers, Stewie and Zoom, don't really
like those things, but that's OK because
there are plenty of things we all like to do.

We all like to play with our animals,

we all REALLY like to do experiments,

play hide-and-go-seek . . .

. . . and we LOVE to jump on our trampoline.

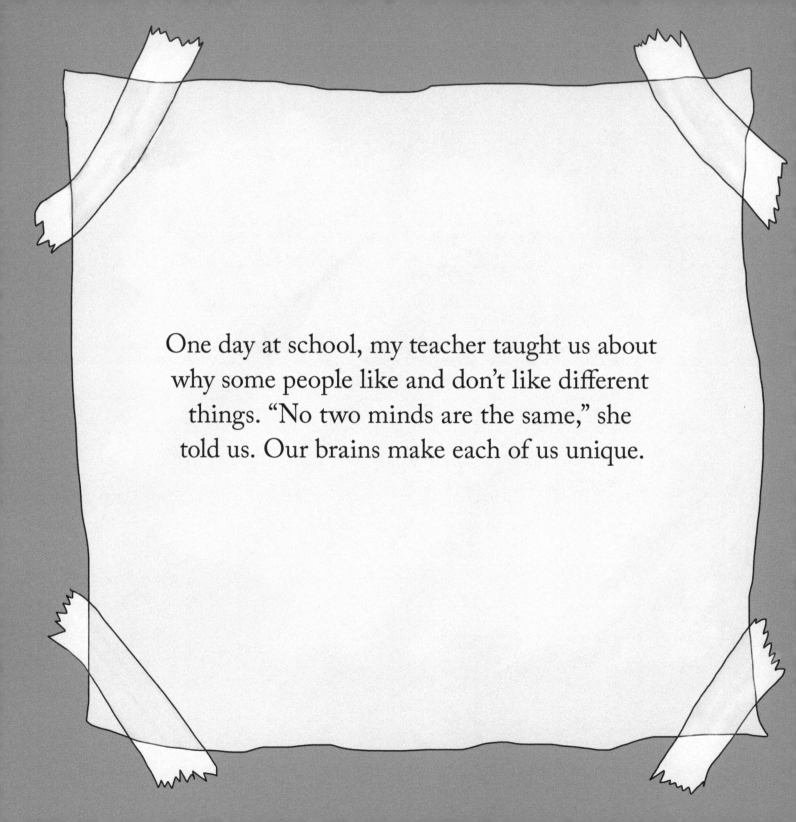

One day at school, my teacher taught us about why some people like and don't like different things. "No two minds are the same," she told us. Our brains make each of us unique.

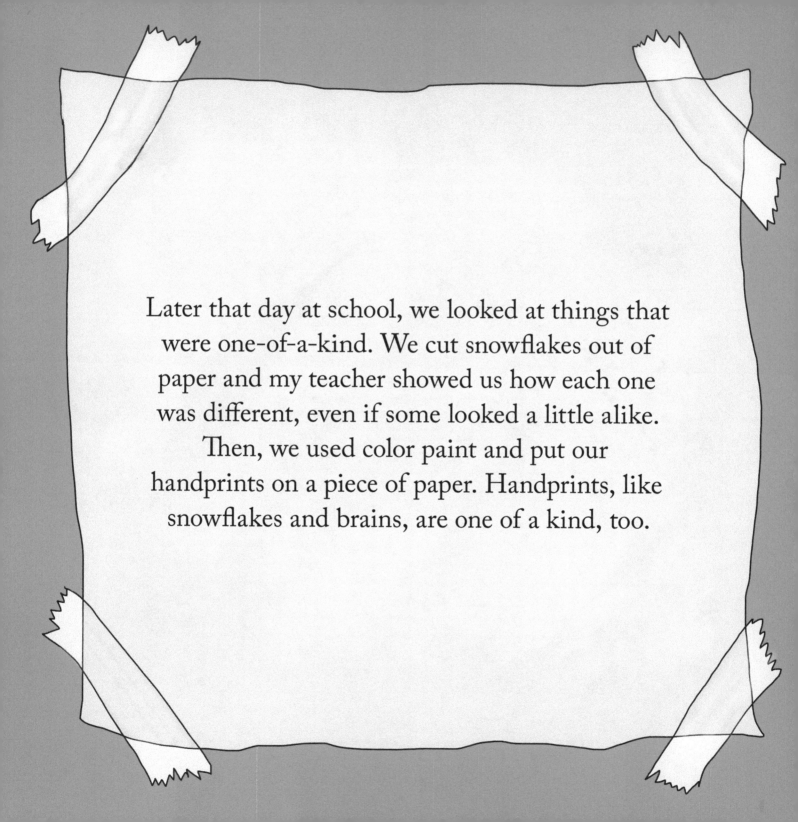

Later that day at school, we looked at things that were one-of-a-kind. We cut snowflakes out of paper and my teacher showed us how each one was different, even if some looked a little alike. Then, we used color paint and put our handprints on a piece of paper. Handprints, like snowflakes and brains, are one of a kind, too.

Our brains control everything we do and everything we like and don't like, teacher told us. "Everyone's mind is something to appreciate, and it is important to have some fun with other kids who may seem to like very different things than you do. I want everyone at recess to play with someone new today."

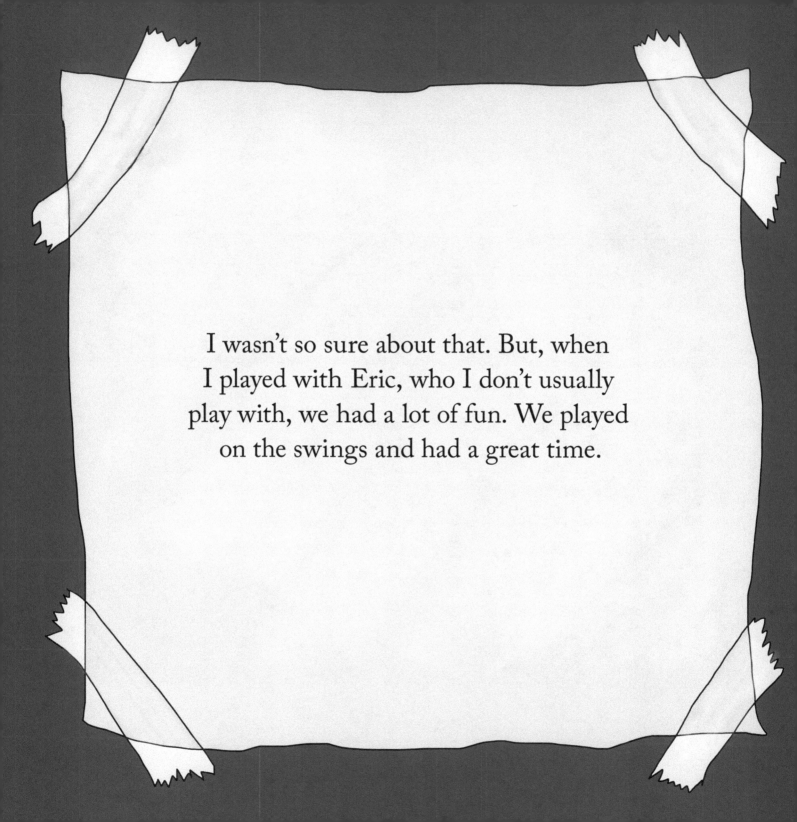

I wasn't so sure about that. But, when I played with Eric, who I don't usually play with, we had a lot of fun. We played on the swings and had a great time.

The next day, Mommy told me Eric was coming over to play. Mommy told us that the handprint of Eric's brain is called "on the spectrum." She told us, "People with these kinds of brains have unique preferences, just like everyone. But, the things they like and don't like might be things we aren't used to. It's very important to play with people who may seem different at first because they can teach us new ways of looking at the world."

That made me think about Eric. He really doesn't like loud noises, so I was worried about him coming over to our booming, loud house. Mommy said, "We will all practice keeping our BOOM! voices low before he comes over. We will use inside voices even when we are outside when Eric is here." It took us a lot of practicing. A really LOT of practicing. Even the dogs tried. Eventually, we got pretty good at using our inside voices.

Once we got good at using quiet voices,
Mommy asked us, "Do you think
you can listen with your eyes?"
"No silly Mommy!" I said.
"No way!" said Stewie.

"Well, paying attention to body language with your eyes is another way of understanding what someone is trying to tell you," Mommy told us. "People's expressions on their faces and the things people do with their bodies are just as important to listen to. Sometimes people react differently to new things than we might expect. So, it is important to pay attention with your eyes as well as your ears."

"People can tell you they are tired, or sad or uncomfortable with just their bodies," Mommy explained.

Mommy made a scared face and covered her ears. "What if I looked like this when you started to yell?" she asked. "I get it!" I yelled. "I can see that you're scared and something is too loud!"

I looked right at Mommy, waved my arms in the air and whispered, "I'm showing you that I'm ready and excited for my play-date." Mommy hugged me tight—showing me with her body how much she loves me.

Daddy and I set out some projects for the play-date and we also practiced being flexible in case Eric wanted to do something else. Daddy practiced doing something else and Stewie and I practiced not pitching a fit. It took some practicing.

The next day, Eric came home with me after school. He flapped his hands and I flapped my fairy wings all the way home. It was so fun.

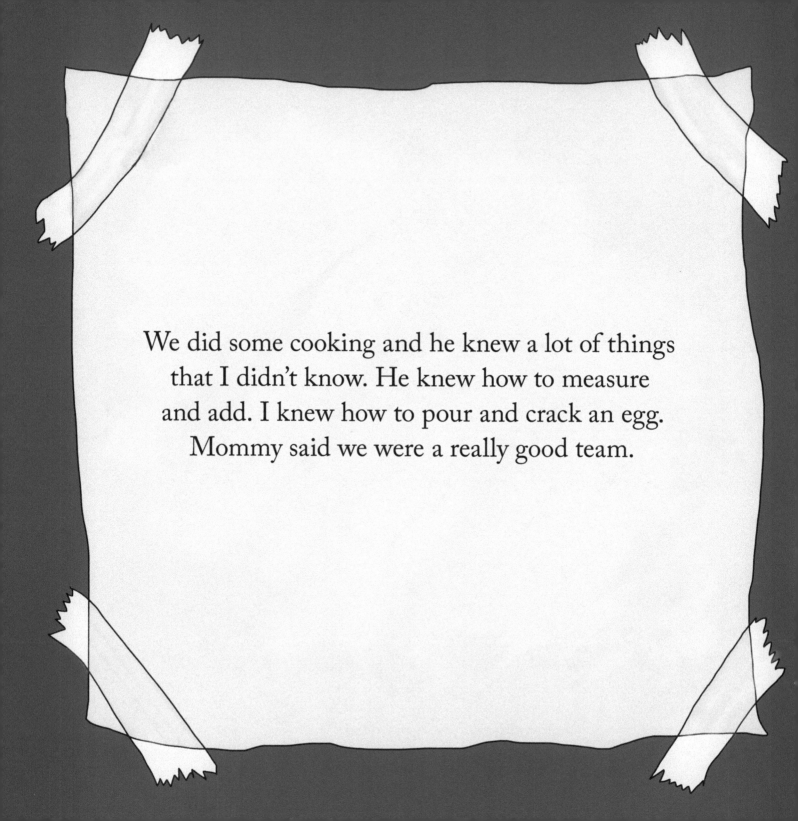

We did some cooking and he knew a lot of things
that I didn't know. He knew how to measure
and add. I knew how to pour and crack an egg.
Mommy said we were a really good team.

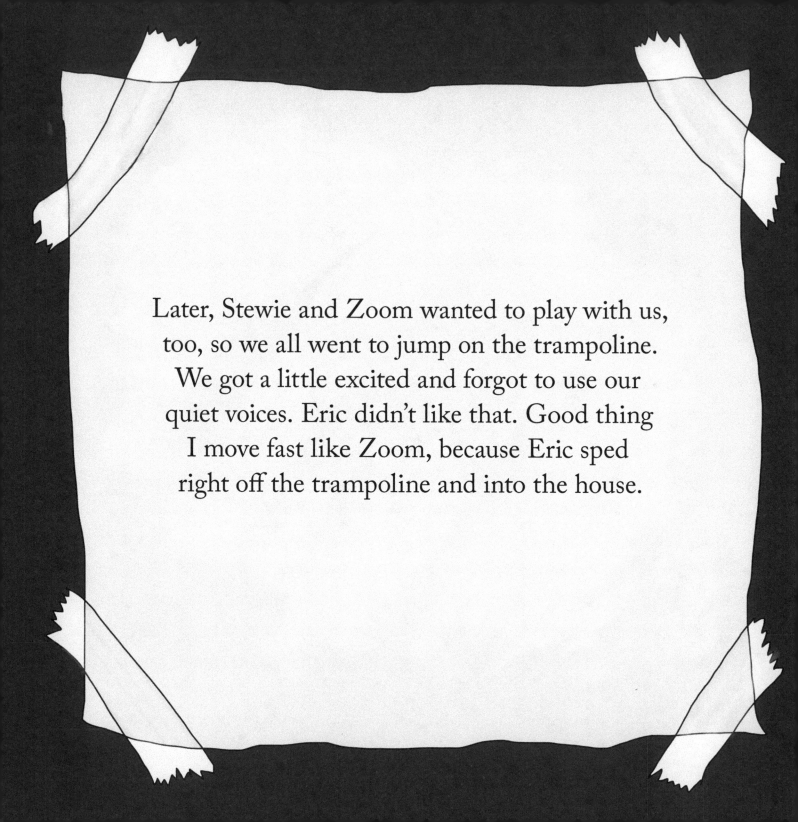

Later, Stewie and Zoom wanted to play with us, too, so we all went to jump on the trampoline. We got a little excited and forgot to use our quiet voices. Eric didn't like that. Good thing I move fast like Zoom, because Eric sped right off the trampoline and into the house.

We all wondered where he was going so we went inside, too. But we couldn't find Eric. When we told Mom we lost Eric, her face was really scary. We looked all over for Eric.

We looked all over the yard.

We looked in the kitchen,

we looked in my room . . .

We finally found Eric right on the couch,
wrapped up super tight in a cozy blanket.
He didn't really want to talk so Mommy said,
"You can all play video games if you want to."

Even Mommy was getting good at being flexible. Eric was really good at video games, so that made him happy. That made us happy, too, because we don't always get to play on screens. Eric taught us a few things about video games. He beat us all! Even Zoom!

When Eric's mom came to pick him up, he didn't want to leave. We didn't want him to leave either. But we all started to use our BOOM! voices and yelled for him to stay. Eric ran out the door to his mom's car. My Mommy said, "It was a great play-date!" I think Eric's Mommy doesn't like loud noises either because it looked like she had a tear in her eye on her way out the door.

I said to Mommy, "Next time we will have
to work much harder at remembering our
quiet voices." But Mommy told me not to
worry, we would remember next time. She
said, "All that really matters is that we all had
fun together. Eric's Mommy was just really,
really happy he had a great first play-date."

Tips to welcome
Special Needs (SN) families for a play-date:

1. It is always best to start with short play-dates. Thirty minutes to an hour is plenty of time to start. It's always good to leave them wanting another play-date!

2. Ask what you should know. A simple email or text to ask if there is anything you should know or if there is anything you can do to set the kids up for a successful time together will do the trick. This would be a wonderful gesture to a parent.

3. Be mindful of sensory sensitivities. If a child is sensitive to sounds, it may be best to run the dishwasher at a later time. If you have a dog, perhaps they can rest in another room until you are sure the child won't be frightened. If bright lights are bothersome, perhaps you can draw the curtains a bit to cut any glare.

4. Consider food allergies and sensitivities. Some parents may love a large, lavish cheese platter. This could be a nightmare for special needs parents as their kids may want to eat all the goodies and there may be allergies.

5. If you are inviting SN kids to a birthday party, send a separate note to parents asking how you can help their child have fun. Perhaps you can invite them to come a bit earlier, have a quiet space for them to retreat to and/or have some treats that meet their dietary restrictions.

6. Build your friendship with SN parents. Special needs parents love and cherish their child just as you do. Being a friend is an incredibly invaluable gift to a special needs parent. At times, having a special needs child can feel isolating.

7. Put away toys or items that can be broken. Nothing will damage a budding friendship more than a favorite toy being broken.

8. If possible, plan the first few play dates at the home of the child with special needs. This relieves the pressure of adapting to a new environment in addition to social pressure.

9. It's OK for your child to be reserved at first. While we want our kids to play, it's fine if they don't at first. As long as everyone is respectful, it's OK for them to do their own thing.

10. Communicate with your kids about their friend's differences and ways in which they are the same. Keep the conversation going after play dates to see how they felt it went, what could be done differently the next time or what you can do again.

Tips for
Special Needs families:

1. Take advantage of opportunities to build your community. At times, it may seem like there isn't anyone who can understand what you are going through, but there are people who care and want to be a part of your community. Start off with small talk and slowly get to know the families around you.

2. Don't pressure yourself too much to make play-dates work. Some will work and some won't. What's important is giving yourself and your kids the opportunity to build relationships. If it doesn't work out, you can try a different play-date at a later time.

3. Don't be hard on yourself. If you aren't up to making new friends, that's OK, too! The most important thing is that you take care of yourself.

4. Build a genuine friendship with parents so you can be relaxed during play-dates. Find a common goal and work together. School fundraisers or other organizations that allow you to work together and get to know each other outside of the kids are good. It helps when the kids see their parents as friends with each other.

5. Allow your child to be themselves. It can be stressful when you are expecting a certain type of interaction. Remember that all kids hang out and/or play differently.

6. Ask for things that will help make it a successful play-date. If the dog barking will frighten your child, ask if the dog can remain outside. Don't expect them to know or understand your child's needs. Instead, let them know what would help make it a successful visit.

7. Explain why you do certain things for your kids. It helps for others to understand what you do and why you do it. It ultimately helps others to understand your child and perhaps they can also accommodate in their own ways.

8. Facilitate but don't force interactions. It's OK for your child to retreat to their room and/or seek breaks throughout the play-date. Make sure their typical friend understands that this isn't personal and at times social situations can be overwhelming.

9. Conquer your fear of rejection. Trying to make friends for yourself and your kids comes with some rejection. This is true for all mom groups. Know that each time is a new opportunity for a budding relationship. Don't give up!

10. Take the pressure off of yourself and your kids. Successful play-dates will look differently to different kids. Some of my best memories are sitting on the couch with a girlfriend watching the TV on mute. It didn't make sense to anyone else, but it did to us.

Mitra Ahani, CCC-SLP—Founder of Thrive Therapy & Social Center in San Jose, CA

Color in the stars
when you have tried each friendship goal:

⭐ I had a play-date with someone new

⭐ I played or ate lunch with someone new today at school

⭐ I played or ate lunch with someone who was alone at school

⭐ I asked someone new to join a group or game

⭐ I practiced understanding with someone today who did something that seemed different

The BOOM! Friendship Award!

This award proudly goes to:

_____

For completing all of the friendship accomplishments!

_____   _____
Date   Parent or Teacher